To those exploring these pages, may this workbook be your guide to a fulfilling retirement journey.

- Toni & Jennifer

MEET THE AUTHORS

Antoinette Petrillo and Jennifer Rovet are professional coaches who specialize in retirement planning for individuals entering retirement. Each of the authors was at a different age and at a different stage of life when they realized the acute need for a service such as this. Both were aware of changing demographics and the increasing proportion of the population entering retirement with little guidance to direct them.

Antoinette Petrillo is a retired financial executive with over 25 years of experience building and leading teams. Having worked for 36 years in the industry, she eagerly awaited her retirement day and as she shut her office door for the last time, was overwhelmed by the emotions that overcame her.

The work that had been so integral to her daily existence, had now reached its end, marking abruptly the conclusion of this phase of her life journey. Facing uncertainty about her next steps, she recognized a notable scarcity of resources tailored for corporate professionals, including herself, navigating the transition into retirement. Having embarked on her journey, she became a Certified Professional Coach, launching her private coaching practice, where she developed her signature program "Intentional Retirement Program". This unique program guides individuals to move forward, emphasizing the possibilities ahead rather than dwelling on what they left behind.

Jennifer Rovet, is a human resources specialist who places retired Canadians in volunteer positions that utilize their unique specialties. Noting firsthand the struggles many of the retirees were undergoing and wanting to better help them, she discovered the new and unique field of retirement coaching. She subsequently became a Certified Professional Retirement Coach and started her own company, Retire Ready Canada to help prospective retirees plan their ideal retirement. Many of the individuals she has coached were initially lost and confused, claiming to lack the sense of purpose they once had and feeling their worlds vastly shrinking. Her program of self-directed planning has allowed them to discover what route to take. Initially, Jennifer's foray was personal, inspired by the plight of her parents with long professional careers enter and enjoy their retirements. Since then, Jennifer has similarly helped individuals from different fields, locales, and even countries find a satisfying retirement path. Jennifer has been featured in articles on retirement in media such as the Globe and Mail, Zoomer Magazine, Good Times Magazine and, http://Mindbodygreen.com. She has also been an executive contributor for Brainz Magazine.

>> Table of Contents

Introduction

Congratulations on purchasing the **Reach For Retirement** workbook. This is the first step towards designing your perfect retirement lifestyle. This workbook was carefully created by Antoinette Petrillo and Jennifer Rovet, two retirement coaches who had a vision of collaborating and using this workbook to complement their coaching services and provide a wealth of resources and exercises for their clients and others to explore.

Retirement means many different things for different people. Some are excited at the prospect of no longer waking up to an alarm clock each day and going to work, being bound by a schedule and days filled with meetings. They can't wait to dive into activities and hobbies they once didn't have time for and be able to spend more time with family and friends. Others, however, feel anxious, scared, and worried about what the future will hold for them. The unknown of retirement can be daunting for so many people and it fills them with many emotions that they don't know how to deal with, where to turn to for help, or who to speak with.

The word retirement often gets a bad rap, and many people believe it conjures up images of life ending and ceasing to exist. However, it is here to stay and must be viewed and understood as not the end of life but the start of something new, a new stage of life.

If planned properly, retirement can be a wonderful time and can allow you to do all the things you want to do, spend time with loved ones and friends and have adventures that you never thought were possible. But it all starts with planning and putting in the work needed to create and design the life you want to live.

Good luck and enjoy!

The 5 Stages of Retirement

Retirement, just like any other major life change, is a journey, and it can take some time to adjust to your new life. There are five distinct stages that you will experience. It's important to understand these stages so you can recognize which one you are in and what you need to do to move forward throughout this stage of life and find satisfaction.

Stage 1: Pre-retirement
Stage 2: The honeymoon phase
Stage 3: Disenchantment
Stage 4: Re-orientation and finding yourself
Stage 5: Stability

Pre-retirement

Pre-retirement is the stage before you retire, which could be anywhere from 5 to 10 years before your big day. During this time, people begin to seriously think about their financial planning and what they need to do to be financially healthy. Planning for your financial future is important, but you must also consider the emotional aspects of retirement. Start thinking about what will make you happy and fulfilled. You may consider moving to a different city or country, downsizing or traveling.

This stage is filled with excitement and anticipation for the next chapter in your life, but it can also be filled with worry and doubt, so taking the time and effort to plan for your financial future, as well as your emotional future, can make the transition into retirement a lot easier.

The honeymoon phase

At last, freedom!! This phase brings with it excitement and newfound freedom along with a sense of relief from the demands of the working world. While this phase can extend beyond 2 years, depending on how you decide to spend your time, it normally lasts between 1-2 years.

This phase also sparks the desire to rekindle relationships with friends and family, pursue hobbies and passions and simply enjoy this time to do whatever brings you happiness.

The 5 Stages of Retirement

Disenchantment

Following the initial euphoria, which brings an end to the honeymoon phase, some retirees may experience a sense of disappointment and disenchantment with their retired life. Retirement is often eagerly anticipated and met with great excitement, but as time passes, the initial thrill may give way to a sense of lessened enthusiasm. It wasn't exactly how you imagined life would be.

This shift can bring about emotions such as loneliness, boredom, depression, and a perceived loss of purpose.

Re-orientation and finding yourself

In line with any life transition, you gradually adapt to your new circumstances and chart your course through this next stage. This phase of retirement, often the most demanding, involves the journey of self-discovery and rediscovering your purpose and identity, requiring both time and deliberate effort. Despite its intricacies, it's also one of the most rewarding and fulfilling stages.

This stage is the ideal time to explore uncharted territories, nurture new hobbies, or rekindle old ones and dive into life's purpose. Free of any full-time work commitments, discovering a sense of purpose may prove to be challenging. Nonetheless, it's crucial to unearth something that reignites your enthusiasm, whether it's volunteer work, spending time with your family, or simply infusing your daily routine with enjoyable and enriching activities.

Stability

The final stage of retirement welcomes a profound sense of contentment, positivity, and happiness in your new life. It's a phase where you may find yourself seamlessly going about your daily routine and lifestyle, engaging in activities that ignite your passion and fill you with a sense of satisfaction. During this time, you savor life with a renewed sense of purpose, gratitude, and a redefined identity.

The Importance of Retirement Lifestyle Planning

Traditionally, retirement planning has focused on financial aspects such as retirement savings, net worth, and investments. While financial planning is very necessary, it's important to recognize that retirement planning is a multi-faceted endeavor that goes beyond financial preparedness.

Consider this: Retirement involves two forms of spending - time and money. Therefore, a comprehensive retirement plan should encompass lifestyle planning alongside traditional financial planning. In reality, several critical components contribute to your retirement success, and finances are just one piece of the puzzle. The other pieces include:

- Identity Shift: Managing the transition from your work identity to a new one in retirement. Attitude Towards Retirement: Cultivating a positive and open attitude towards this new phase of life.
- Health and Wellbeing: Prioritizing and maintaining physical and mental health throughout your retirement years.
- Sense of Purpose: Finding and nurturing a sense of purpose and meaning in retirement.
- Activities and Leisure Interests: Identifying and engaging in activities and interests that bring joy and fulfillment.
- Relationship Quality: Evaluating the quality of your relationships with loved ones and friends.
- Replacing Work Benefits: Exploring how to replace the benefits you derived from your work, such as structure and social connections

In essence, a successful retirement plan is a holistic one that considers all these pieces, recognizing that financial stability is just one element of your overall retirement journey.

How this workbook can help you

We created this workbook to help people like yourself address the challenges you may experience as you go through the different stages of retirement and how to create strategies to overcome and conquer those challenges. By using this workbook, you will be asked a series of questions and complete exercises that will help you face head-on the changes that occur during the transition process from your traditional work life and be able to plan out exactly how you want to live your life as you approach this next stage.

The workbook is divided into six chapters – Mindset, Health and Wellness, Purpose, Family and Social Connections Your Identity, and finally, your Retirement Roadmap.

Each chapter will have you think about your life, what it is that you enjoy doing and with whom, how you are feeling now and where you want to be in the future. By the end of the workbook, you should be able to put together a structured plan and vision so you are feeling confident and excited and your interests and passions can be a part of your new retirement life.

You can use this workbook on your own or in conjunction with a Retirement Coach. You can use it while you are still working, as you begin to approach retirement or even a few years into your retirement. Each chapter of this workbook can be done on its own and completed in the order you prefer, namely those that have meaning for you. You may even want to complete some chapters before you decide to retire and then redo them after you have retired. Completing certain chapters prior to retirement may be helpful to your pre-planning while preferring to only address certain aspects after you have fully retired. It's totally up to you.

It's important to remember that everyone is unique, and everyone's retirement will look and feel different. Retirement planning takes time and commitment. It requires a deep dive into your life to discover what it is you enjoy and what you want to do in this next stage of your life.

Remember, it's your retirement; we just want to make sure it's the best one possible!

The first step in your journey is understanding who you are today and what your vision is for your retirement years. By knowing yourself, you can better plan for what you want and need, which will lead to a fulfilling and rewarding future.

The more you can get to know yourself before retirement, the better you can plan for your wants and needs in retirement. This is the time when you have the opportunity for some completely new experiences that may reveal a side of yourself that you never knew existed.

Are you ready for

retirement?

MINDSET
Retirement Readiness

Understanding how prepared you are when you make the decision to retire will help you better design your roadmap moving forward. This will help guide you and discover which areas of your life need some work to establish a successful retirement transition.

Refer to the statements below and indicate your level of satisfaction and happiness in each area.
1 = Least satisfied and/or happy and   5 = Most satisfied and/or happy

	1	2	3	4	5
I have an identity and purpose outside of my job.	○	○	○	○	○
I have a social network that's not tied to my job.	○	○	○	○	○
My family relationships are good.	○	○	○	○	○
I like the lifestyle I am living now.	○	○	○	○	○
I have a vision for my retirement life.	○	○	○	○	○
I have passions and hobbies.	○	○	○	○	○
When I set goals, I achieve them.	○	○	○	○	○
I have activities that keep me busy.	○	○	○	○	○
I am in good physical and mental health.	○	○	○	○	○

MINDSET
Life Essentials

If you were starting a new life today, what would you absolutely require? What are your priorities, and what do you value most?

In the clouds below, write your life essentials. Then, think about how you can use your retirement years to build a purposeful future based on your life essentials.

After dedicating considerable time to self-discovery and identifying your values and priorities, it's time to pivot your attention toward other critical aspects that contribute to a joyful retirement.

Let's now concentrate on factors like maintaining good health and physical fitness. As you progress in your retirement journey, it becomes crucial to embrace a well-rounded lifestyle. Achieving balance and good health in your life is the pathway to lasting happiness.

What are your health &

wellness goals?

HEALTH & WELLNESS
Gauge Your Health Plan

Maintaining a healthy lifestyle in retirement is vital. Your health is your wealth.
Gauge your overall health by answering the questions below.

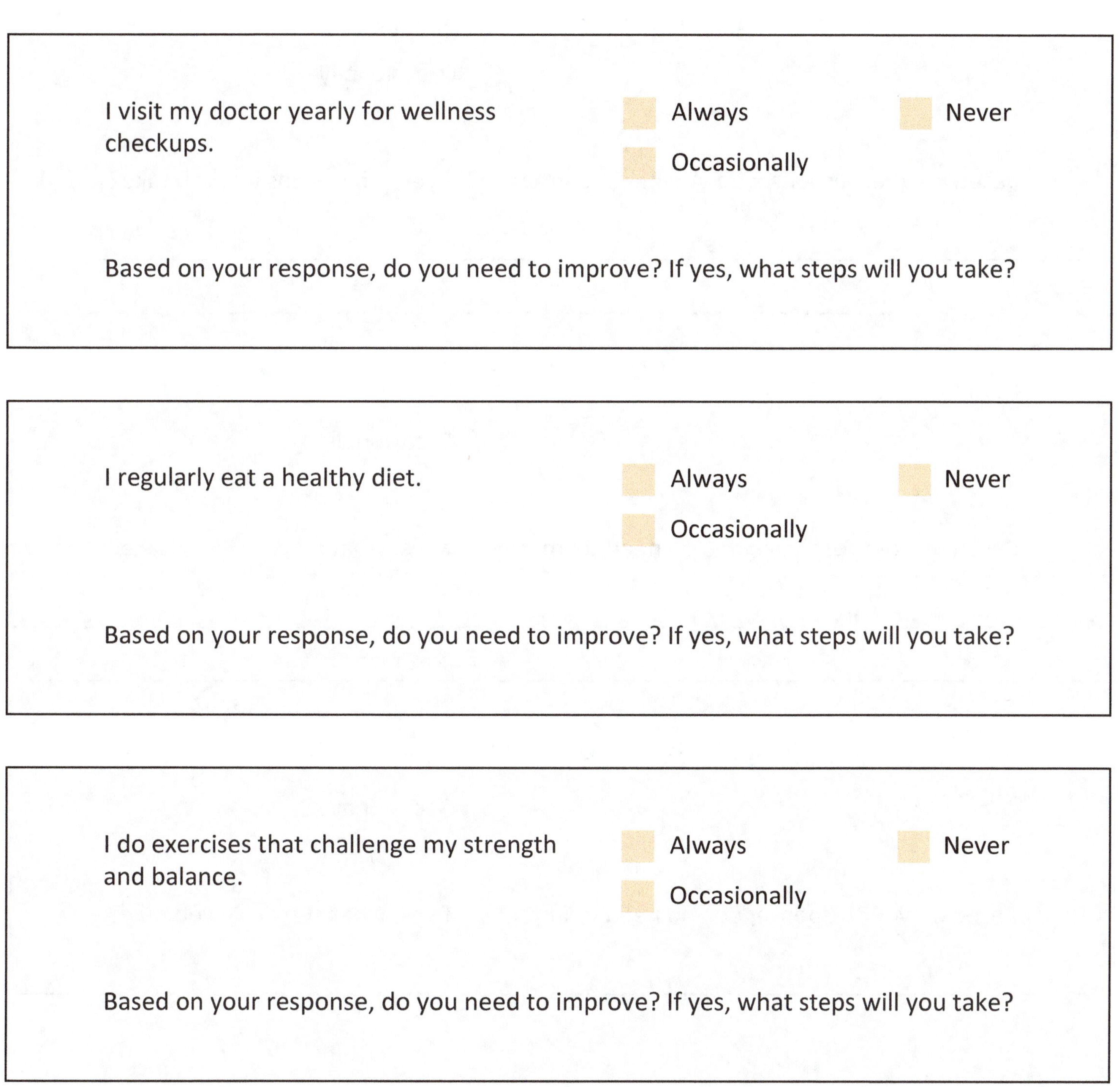

I visit my doctor yearly for wellness checkups.

☐ Always   ☐ Never
☐ Occasionally

Based on your response, do you need to improve? If yes, what steps will you take?

I regularly eat a healthy diet.

☐ Always   ☐ Never
☐ Occasionally

Based on your response, do you need to improve? If yes, what steps will you take?

I do exercises that challenge my strength and balance.

☐ Always   ☐ Never
☐ Occasionally

Based on your response, do you need to improve? If yes, what steps will you take?

HEALTH & WELLNESS
Gauge Your Health Plan

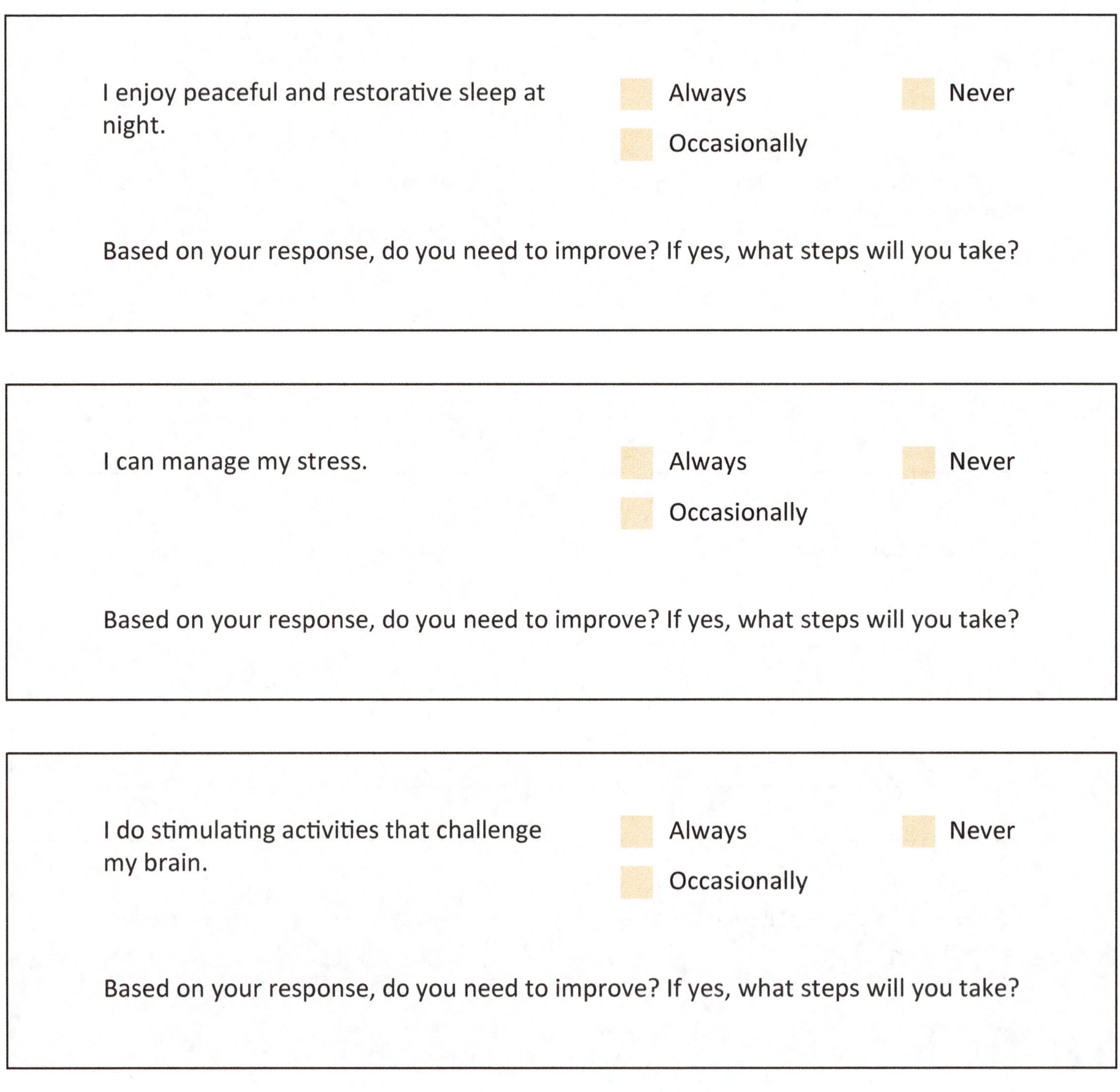

I enjoy peaceful and restorative sleep at night.

☐ Always   ☐ Never

☐ Occasionally

Based on your response, do you need to improve? If yes, what steps will you take?

I can manage my stress.

☐ Always   ☐ Never

☐ Occasionally

Based on your response, do you need to improve? If yes, what steps will you take?

I do stimulating activities that challenge my brain.

☐ Always   ☐ Never

☐ Occasionally

Based on your response, do you need to improve? If yes, what steps will you take?

HEALTH & WELLNESS
Mastering Change

Retirement, being one of life's significant transitions, often evokes a sense of uncertainty and apprehension. Just like other life changes we've encountered, it can be challenging for various reasons, including fear of the unfamiliar, stepping beyond our comfort zone, a perceived loss of control, a dip in self-confidence, or feelings of loss and grief.

Reflect on a recent situation and answer the questions below to help you master your own change as you transition into this new stage of life.

Describe a time when you feared not knowing the outcome of a new situation.

Describe the actual outcome and how you overcame that fear.

How might you use this prior experience to help overcome your retirement fears?

HEALTH & WELLNESS
Express Your Gratitude

Being able to retire is a priviledge and wonderful opportunity. Being thankful and showing gratitude helps cultivate a positive attitude. And a positive attitude is essential for living a long life. Take some time to reflect on why this phase of life is so special and what the next chapter means to you.

List three reasons why you are grateful for retirement

1.

2.

3.

Stay Optimistic!

Complete these statements with words or phrases to keep yourself encouraged about the future.

I believe my retirement will be...

What matters most to me is..

I will stay relevant in retirement by...

It's wonderful to transition from a hectic working life to the relaxed retirement lifestyle. Two key factors for a fulfilling retirement are having ample financial resources and meaningful pursuits to look forward to. While you might possess the financial means and a list of engaging hobbies, they alone may not guarantee true satisfaction in retirement. What could be crucial is discovering a profound sense of purpose that drives your retirement years.

What is my purpose in retirement?

PURPOSE
What's Your Preference?

To get a general idea of how best to organize your day, begin with understanding your preferences.

On a scale of 1 to 10, with 1 being not at all, 5 being neutral and 10 being very much, rate each of the following statements.

I like to have a set routine to follow.

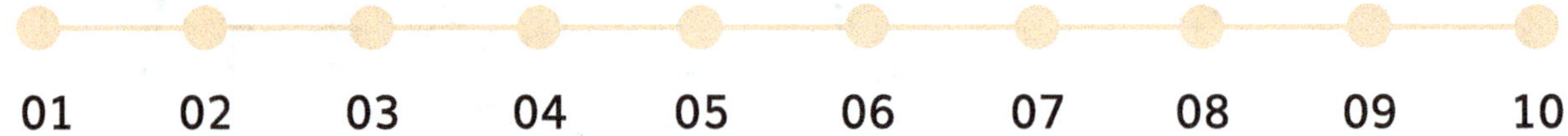

01   02   03   04   05   06   07   08   09   10

I get bored if I'm not busy.

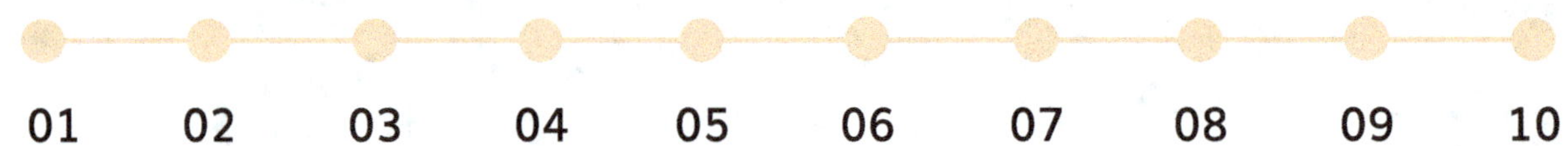

01   02   03   04   05   06   07   08   09   10

It's important for me to accomplish something daily/weekly.

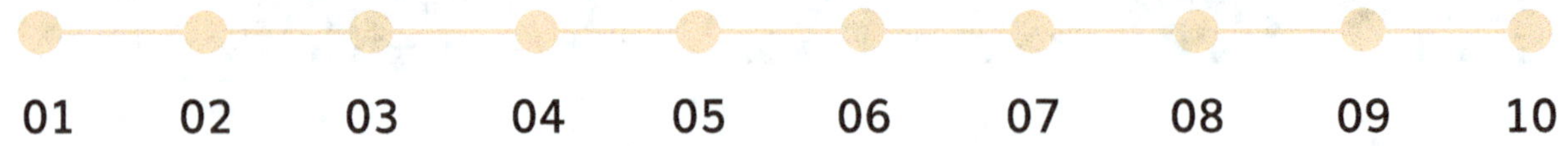

01   02   03   04   05   06   07   08   09   10

I like to have alone time throughout the day.

01   02   03   04   05   06   07   08   09   10

PURPOSE

What Are You Curious About?

The need to make a living sometimes prevents us from doing the fun things we want to do or enjoyed doing as children.

As you approach retirement, think about activities you were curious about as a child and now as an adult. Review and reply to each of the questions below.

What did you enjoy doing as a child?

I loved to:

Because:

What activities do you enjoy doing as an adult but have not had the time or opportunity to explore?

I loved to:

Because:

List three activities you would like to do during retirement:

I loved to:

Because:

PURPOSE
My Ideal Retirement Week

What would your perfect retirement week look like? How would you spend your days? Who would you be socializing with? What activities or hobbies would you like to try or rekindle?

How you spend your retirement days is how you will spend your retirement life. In the tables below, indicate how you would like to spend each day while in retirement.

MONDAY	TUESDAY
☐	☐
☐	☐
☐	☐

WEDNESDAY	THURSDAY
☐	☐
☐	☐
☐	☐

FRIDAY	SATURDAY & SUNDAY
☐	☐
☐	☐
☐	☐

PURPOSE

What Do You Miss?

The shift from work to retirement isn't an immediate switch. Retirement doesn't automatically erase your work-related thoughts and propel you into a retirement mindset.

This exercise aims to identify the elements in your work that bring or brought you joy and explore strategies to navigate beyond those moments. Reflect on the aspects of your work that you find or found fulfilling, and jot down your thoughts in the space provided below.

WHAT I MISS or THINK I WILL MISS	WHY I MISS IT OR WILL MISS IT	WHAT CAN REPLACE IT

PURPOSE
Finding Your IKIGAI

Discovering purpose in life represents one of our most fundamental human needs, yet we often struggle to uncover our true desires. The Japanese concept of ikigai can assist in this journey. While it lacks a precise translation, ikigai can be considered your 'reason for being', the essence that gives life its meaning.

Your ikigai resides at the intersection of your passions and talents, aligning with what others require and are willing to value.

Uncovering your ikigai not only enriches your life with deeper meaning and purpose but also fosters improved physical health and mental well-being.

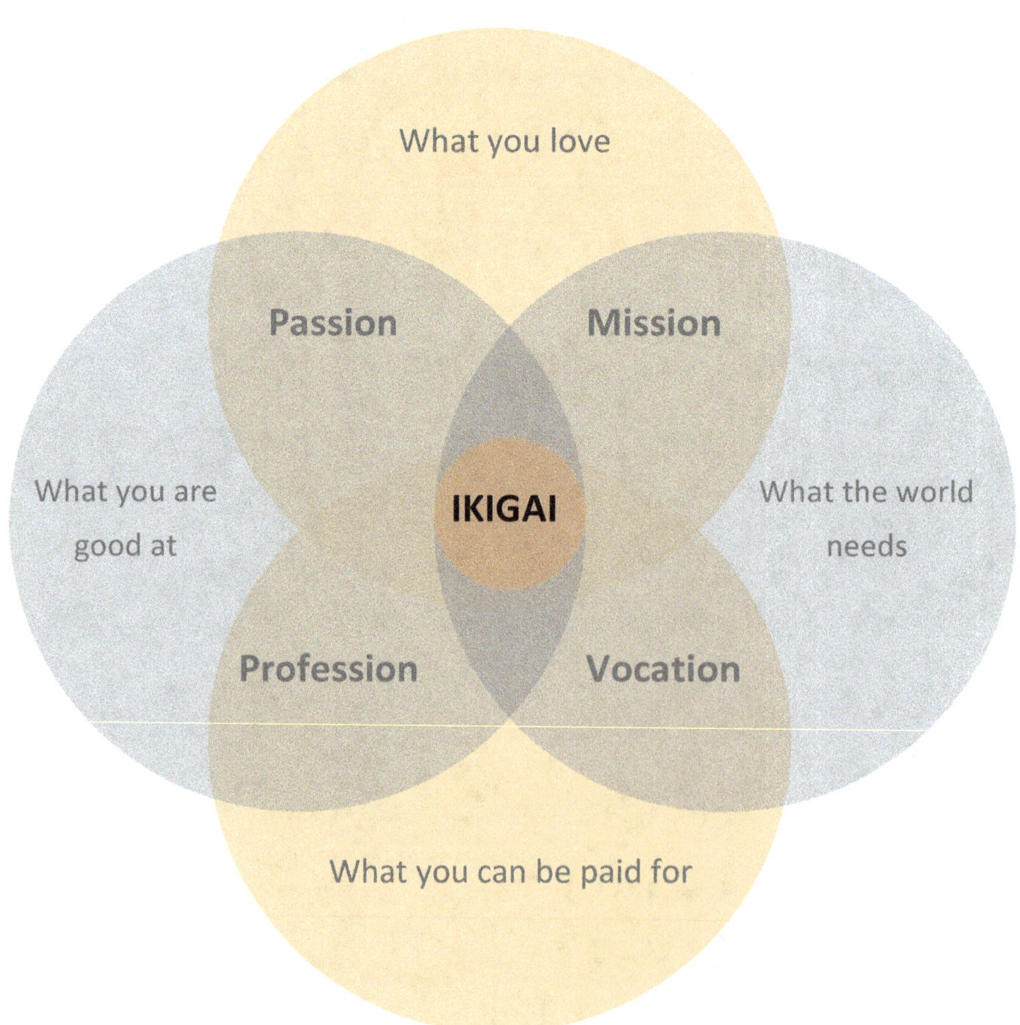

PURPOSE
Finding Your IKIGAI

To understand the diagram, ask yourself these four questions:

1. What do you love, and what are you good at? This is your **PASSION**.
2. What do you love, and what is something that the world needs? This is your **MISSION**.
3. What is something you are good at and can get paid for? This is your **PROFESSION**.
4. What is something you can get paid for, and is something the world needs? This is your **VOCATION**.

Let's explore each question and how they can help you find your **ikigai**.

What do you love?
This is the gut feeling you have about the things that you truly enjoy doing and puts you into a state of flow. For many people, this can be artistic and creative endeavors such as reading, writing, and filmmaking, but it is certainly not limited to this.

What are you good at?
This is not simply a natural gift or talent. These are the things you are curious about, things you can work at and develop your skills so that you eventually become great at them.

What the world needs?
This means that you can provide value to others through your talents or services. Leaning into this will allow you to make a difference in some way and have an impact.

What can you get paid for?
If there is something you are good at and want to continue, you could find a way to make it financially sustainable. By doing that, you check off a major component of your happiness: the freedom to do what you want without worrying about how you are going to make ends meet or just making a little extra money.

PURPOSE
IKIGAI Exercise

Now that you understand how the concept of ikigai works, take some time to fill in each section and answer the questions. Once you have done that, you will be able to complete the sentence "My **ikigai** is..."

PASSION

What do you love?

What are you good at?

MISSION

What do you love?

What is something the world needs?

PROFESSION

What are you good at?

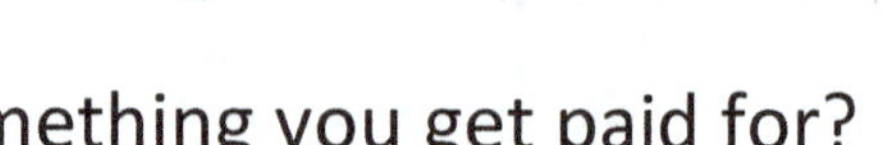

Something you get paid for?

VOCATION

What is something the world needs?

Something you get paid for?

MY IKIGAI IS ...

PURPOSE
Purpose Statement

Memories and experiences can profoundly affect our lives, sometimes without even realizing it. For this exercise, reflect on your past and write down 5 very specific and vivid memories. These memories are not limited to your career but can be from any time in your life.

- Be as specific and descriptive as you can, including how you felt, who else was there, and what happened.
- Think of specific experiences and people that have shaped you.
- The memories don't always have to be positive; sometimes, negative experiences profoundly impact our lives.
- Don't overanalyze at this point; just write down your most meaningful memories.

PURPOSE
Purpose Statement - Cont'd

Your purpose will come from your feelings around these memories, not what actually happened. Here are some questions to ask yourself for each memory. Once you have finished, try to write your 'purpose statement'. Your purpose statement will help guide your path and journey during your retirement years.

v v v

How did that memory make you feel?

What was it about that memory and experience that you loved best?

How did that memory affect you and who you have become today?

Can you identify any theme(s) from your memories? Circle any common words that you see in each memory that you wrote down. For example, help, teach, guide, or mentor.

Now try to write out your Purpose Statement:

To _____________________ (contribution) so that _____________________ (impact on others)

Your contribution phrase is usually a verb + person.
Your impact phrase is usually a state of being.

Maintaining a vibrant social life during retirement is vital for your overall happiness and well-being. If the majority of your social interactions were work-related, forging new connections could present a unique set of challenges.

Engaging with your family, friends, colleagues, and like-minded individuals who share your interests can be incredibly fulfilling.

How will I maintain social connections?

SOCIAL CONNECTIONS
Family Time

Staying connected to your family members is important throughout your retirement years. This means more than just staying in touch through texting and social media. It's important to start nurturing your family relationships even before you retire.

In the diagram below, write a statement for each of the five family members stating how you will stay connected. For example, you may want to visit your grandchildren every weekend.

PARENTS

____

____

CHILDREN

MY FAMILY

SIBLINGS

____

____

GRAND CHILDREN

EXTENDED FAMILY

SOCIAL CONNECTIONS
Social Portfolio

Just as a financial portfolio addresses your financial well-being, a social portfolio addresses your social and emotional well-being. Your social portfolio might be a mix of family, new and old friends, and engaging activities to do with these people.

Take some time to reflect on your social portfolio and answer the three questions below.

How secure is your social portfolio? (Do you have meaningful relationships? Are you involved in enjoyable activities?)

Have you diversified your social portfolio? (Do you have things you like to do alone and other activities that get you out with people?)

What can you do to increase and diversify your social portfolio? (Where can you meet new people and get involved in activities?)

SOCIAL CONNECTIONS
Who are Your Friends?

What are social connections, and why are they important in retirement? Social connections are all the people in your life that you love spending time with. The quality and uniqueness of these connections, whether they are family members or close friends, can have a profound effect on your transition into retirement and all the years that follow.

List below the social connections you wish to maintain or grow during your retirement years. This list could include current friends, work friends, and even old friends.

SOCIAL CONNECTIONS
Your Social Calendar

Part of being social is being intentional and committed to getting out of your house and spending time with people. This could be, for example, going out for a regular lunch with a friend or joining a monthly book club. Social interaction, no matter what it is, is beneficial for your health and overall well-being.

Take a moment to reflect and pinpoint the activities that bring you joy or interest you, and proceed to fill in your social calendar below.

JANUARY	FEBRUARY	MARCH
APRIL	MAY	JUNE
JULY	AUGUST	SEPTEMBER
OCTOBER	NOVEMBER	DECEMBER

Chapter 5: Your Identity

Your work has played a significant role in shaping the person you are today. It may have provided you with a sense of value, accomplishment, recognition, purpose, and financial security. Now that your career is no longer the primary source of these feelings or needs, you face the task of finding new motivations to start each day.

The exercises in this section are designed to guide your reflection on your past and present so you can better understand yourself and start shaping your retirement identity.

Who am I after retirement?

IDENTITY
WHO AM I WITHOUT A JOB TITLE?

Giving up your work identity is one of the most challenging parts of retirement. Many retirees struggle with this. As you prepare for retirement, this may be the ideal time to discover, or rediscover, who you are, and what makes you "you".

Review the questions below and provide your response for each one.

What role does work and your job title play in how you define yourself?

How would you describe yourself if you couldn't refer to a job title or an occupation?

How can your outside interests replace your work identity and help create a new identity?

IDENTITY
Finding Your Energy Source

How do you discover your work's energy source? Think about the parts of your work you enjoy or did enjoy most. Are you energized by having a specific job title, by engaging in team activities, communicating and leading, or by the feeling that what you are doing has great importance?

Review the questions below to identify your energy source. Once you have identified it, you will know what it is that you'll want to keep so that you are happy in retirement.

What part of your work fuels your energy source?

How can you continue to be fueled by this source in your retirement?

IDENTITY
My Values and Strengths

Many of us mistakenly conclude that having paid employment or a job title defines who we are. Instead, ask yourself, "What value do I or did I bring to my job?"

Using the boxes below, capture the strengths that you acquired throughout your working years and how you can include them in your retirement life so you'll have meaning and fulfillment.

MY STRENGTH IS

I CAN USE IT TO

MY STRENGTH IS

I CAN USE IT TO

MY STRENGTH IS

I CAN USE IT TO

Chapter 6: Retirement Lifestyle Plan

Throughout the course of this workbook, you've actively engaged in a series of exercises designed to uncover your interests, passions, and strategies for maintaining a fulfilling and balanced retirement lifestyle.

Now is the perfect time to combine these insights into a unified tapestry of short and long-term retirement goals. Your goals act as a guiding light, providing clarity, motivation, and the pathway to actualizing the retirement life you've envisioned.

What is my Retirement Lifestyle Plan?

Retirement Lifestyle Plan
Part 1: WHAT

As you have been working through these exercises, you've thought a lot about how you want your life to unfold. As you continue to reflect, summarize what areas are going well and identify what needs improvement. Capture this information in the table below.

HEALTH & WELLNESS	SOCIAL CONNECTIONS
Going Well: Needs Improvement:	Going Well: Needs Improvement:
IDENTITY	**PURPOSE & MEANING**
Going Well: Needs Improvement:	Going Well: Needs Improvement:

Retirement Lifestyle Plan
Part 2: HOW

Now that you've identified what areas of your retirement need improvement, in the table below identify how implementing 2 or 3 strategies will help you reach your goals.

HEALTH & WELLNESS	SOCIAL CONNECTIONS
IDENTITY	**PURPOSE & MEANING**

Retirement Lifestyle Plan
Part 3: WHY

As you identify areas that require improvement, ask yourself, "Why am I doing this?" Your "Why" is the driving force to keep you motivated. Not knowing your "why" can lead to outcomes such as indecisiveness, procrastination, self-doubt, fear of failure and inconsistency.

Name one retirement goal you identified that you would like to imrpove and describe why this is important to you?

Is your "why" significant enough to motivate you if the goal/task becomes challenging?

How would not completing this goal/task affect your retirement? How would you feel?

Retirement Lifestyle Plan
My Commitment

Now that you've identified your What, How and Why, take some time to outline in each of the boxes below, your committment to implement and sustain your plan.

HEALTH & WELLNESS	SOCIAL CONNECTIONS

IDENTITY	PURPOSE & MEANING

Retirement Lifestyle Plan
My Retirement Plan

As you embarked on your retirement journey, you had a specific vision of your retirement life. After completing these exercises, take a few minutes to reflect how you feel at this point. Now, use the knowledge gained from the exercises to create your personalized retirement plan in the space provided below.

<table>
<tr><td>MY RETIREMENT LIFESTYLE PLAN</td></tr>
<tr><td>

</td></tr>
</table>

CONNECT WITH US!

Congratulations! You've taken proactive measures and invested time to ensure your retirement is well-prepared, allowing you to embrace your best life.

For additional resources, valuable insights, and personalized guidance, we encourage you to explore our individual web sites. Should you require direct assistance, please don't hesitate to reach out to us using the contact information provided below. Your journey to a fulfilling retirement is important, and we're dedicated to being a reliable source of help and support for you.

Happy Retirement!

Jennifer Rovet

🌐 *retirereadycanada.com*

Toni Perillo

🌐 *retirewithintention.com*

 retireready canada@gmail.com

 tonipcoaching@gmail.com

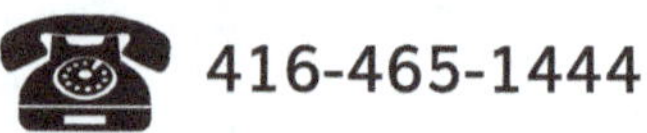 416-465-1444

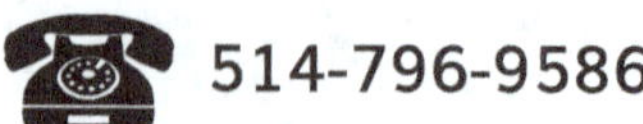 514-796-9586

 linkedin.com/in/jenniferrovet

 linkedin.com/in/antoinette-petrillo-cfp-cpc-27245198

Reach For Retirement

Embark on a journey towards a retirement characterized by optimal health, robust social connections, and a profound sense of purpose!

Welcome to a personalized exploration of self-discovery and empowerment through our meticulously crafted workbook to provide you with the tools and profound insights necessary to create a retirement that aligns with your deepest dreams and aspirations.

This workbook serves as your trusted companion—a step-by-step guide designed to take you on a unique journey. Begin planning for your ideal retirement today and unlock a future teeming with happiness and fulfillment.

As you prepare for retirement, remember that life's most magnificent views follow your greatest climbs